Sleeping Beauty

illustrated by

Sylvia Ward

Sleeping Beauty

NCE UPON A TIME, there lived a King and Queen, who longed for a child more than anything in the world. They were very popular with all the people of the kingdom, so when, after many years, the Queen announced that she was expecting a baby, there was much rejoicing. A few months later, a baby girl was born. The overjoyed parents held a huge feast, and all the lords and ladies from the kingdom were invited

to attend. The Queen invited seven fairies, and asked each of them to be godmother to her daughter. Each fairy was to give the Princess a special magical gift. The fairies were to sit at a special table, right next to the King and Queen. At each place setting, there was a golden plate and a goblet encrusted with jewels. However, there was one fairy in the land that the Queen forgot to invite. When this fairy found out what had happened, she flew into a rage and stormed into the party. The Queen said she was sorry for her mistake, and called for a place to be set for the fairy at the table. But there were no more special plates or goblets left, and the fairy was still furious with the Queen.

The time came for the fairy godmothers to give their special gifts to the baby Princess. The first fairy waved her wand and said, "I give the Princess the gift of beauty."

"I give her goodness to match her beauty," said the second fairy.

"I give her happiness for as long as she shall live," smiled the third.

"She will be a good dancer," said the fourth.

"She will be clever and quick," said the fifth.

The sixth fairy gave the Princess the gift of a beautiful voice. The seventh fairy was just about to give her gift when the forgotten fairy could no longer contain her anger.

"I have a gift too!" spat the forgotten fairy. "My gift is a curse to you and your kingdom for not inviting me to the feast. On this child's sixteenth birthday, she will prick her finger on the spindle of a spinning wheel and die!" And with that, the forgotten fairy gave a screech of laughter before she disappeared into the night.

The King and Queen and all their guests gasped and shook with fear.

"Whatever can we do?" they asked one another. Nobody wanted the Princess to die from a jealous fairy's curse.

"Perhaps I can help," said the lovely seventh fairy, who had been interrupted before giving her gift to the Princess.

"I cannot undo this curse," she said. "But I can make it less terrible. The Princess will not die when she pricks her finger. Instead she will fall into a deep sleep, which will last at least a hundred years. The Princess will awaken only when she receives a kiss from a Prince whose heart is true."

The terrified King and Queen did not find comfort in the fairy's gift. In an attempt to save his precious daughter, the King ordered that every spinning wheel in the land be burned.

Many years passed and the people of the kingdom forgot about the curse. However nobody could forget about the gifts that the other fairies had given the Princess. She was beautiful, kind, clever and thoughtful, and she moved with the grace of a dancer. She was always merry and bright, and she made everyone she met feel full of joy. It was not long before her sixteenth birthday came around, and the King and Queen planned another big celebration to mark the occasion. That morning the Princess had little to do, as everybody else was busy preparing for the celebration. She decided to occupy herself by exploring

parts of the castle she did not know well.

At the top of the tallest tower, she discovered a little room she had never seen before. In this room there sat an old woman spinning thread. The Princess, who had never seen anyone spin before, went over to the old woman and asked her what she was doing.

"I am spinning thread, my sweet," said the old woman, who was really the wicked fairy in disguise.

"How wonderful," said the Princess. "Please may I try?"

"Of course you may," replied the fairy, making way for the Princess in front of the spinning wheel. As soon as the Princess started to spin, her hand slipped and she pricked her finger on

the spindle. At once she fell into a deep sleep. The wicked fairy crowed with delight and fled from the castle.

Soon the King and Queen began to fear that something dreadful had happened to their

daughter. In a terrible panic they searched the castle high and low, until they found her sound asleep in the spinning room. "NO, NO!" cried the King when he saw the Princess slumped on the floor beside the wheel. Nobody in the land could wake the Princess, so they dressed her in

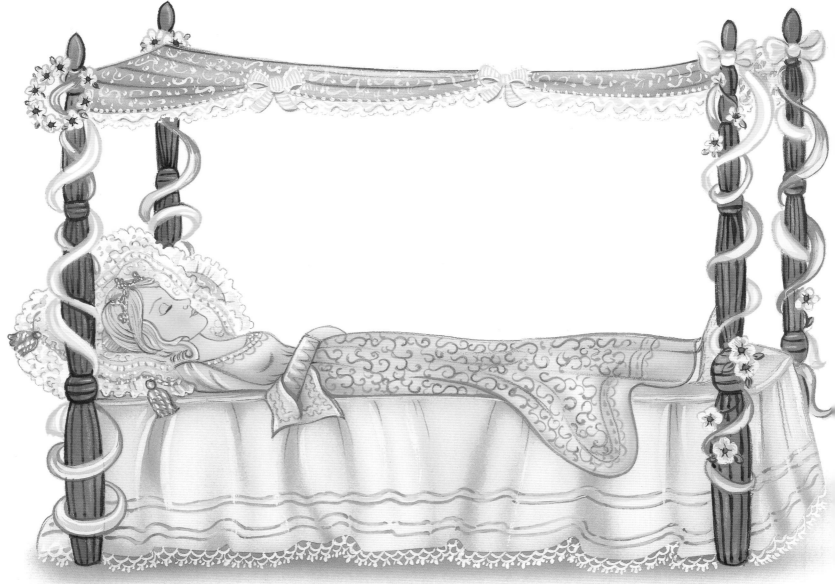

a beautiful nightgown and tucked her into a beautiful bed.

When the seventh fairy heard that the wicked fairy's curse had begun, she rushed to the kingdom. "I know what I must do," she thought to herself. "I must put everybody else in the land to sleep too. Then nobody will suffer, knowing that the Princess cannot be woken. When she does wake, she will still be amongst her friends and family. Nobody will wake until the Princess opens her eyes."

So the seventh fairy flew up and down the kingdom. As she flew, she touched everybody

she saw with her magic wand. She touched all the servants, and the King and Queen. She touched the farmers in the fields. She even touched the animals, so the horses slumbered peacefully in the stables, and the cats lay snuggled next to the very mice they had been trying to catch. Once she was sure everybody was asleep, the fairy waved her magic wand one last time. Suddenly a magical forest, full of thorny trees sprang up around the castle to protect it.

As the years passed, people forgot about the kingdom lost deep in the forest.

One day, many, many years later, a young Prince was out riding around the edge of the forest. Suddenly his horse became restless. The Prince glanced up and something caught his eye. It was the very tip of the tallest turret on the castle. "It looks like there is a kingdom buried in the forest," he thought to himself.

The Prince began to ask everybody he met if they knew about the mystery of the hidden castle, but nobody remembered Sleeping Beauty.

One day, however, the Prince met a very old man who told him that his father had spoken of a Princess who would fall asleep for a hundred years or more. It was the story of Sleeping Beauty.

The Prince made up his mind at once. He decided to fight his way through the thorny and dark forest to rescue the Princess himself. The way was blocked, and the going was hard, but day-by-day, bit-by-bit, the Prince hacked his way through the thorns. He never gave up, no matter how scratched and bruised and weary he became. One day, as the Prince chopped at the thorns, he felt his sword hit something hard. He pulled back the branches to find he had uncovered the gateway to the castle. The Prince rushed bravely into the courtyard.

Everywhere he looked, the ground was covered in snoring bodies. He found the King and Queen slumped peacefully on their thrones, and stable-hands dreaming, propped up by their brooms. At last the Prince found the bedroom

where the Princess had been sleeping for such a long time. He was dazzled by her beauty. Bending down on one knee, he kissed her upon her cheek. Straight away, Sleeping Beauty opened her eyes. When she saw the young man, she smiled and asked him, "Are you the handsome Prince, who has come to rescue me?"

"Yes," replied the Prince, and he told her of his adventures in the dark and thorny forest.

Suddenly a great roar of noise, which came from all around them, startled the two young people. The enchantment had been lifted, and all the people and creatures of the kingdom were awake once more. They heard birds begin to sing, horses neigh and cats meow. It seemed as if life in the kingdom had never been halted at all, now that the Princess was no longer asleep. The King and Queen rose from their thrones and came to find the young couple. They were overjoyed to see their daughter with the Prince, and the King and Queen celebrated with a huge party for everybody.

At the end of the party, the Prince and
the Princess were married, and they all lived
happily ever after in the kingdom that
had been forgotten for so long.

THE END